A Note to Parents and Caregivers:

Read-it! Readers are for children who are just starting on the amazing road to reading. These beautiful books support both the acquisition of reading skills and the love of books.

 The PURPLE LEVEL presents basic topics and objects using high frequency words and simple language patterns.

 The RED LEVEL presents familiar topics using common words and repeating sentence patterns.

 The BLUE LEVEL presents new ideas using a larger vocabulary and varied sentence structure.

 The YELLOW LEVEL presents more challenging ideas, a broad vocabulary, and wide variety in sentence structure.

 The GREEN LEVEL presents more complex ideas, an extended vocabulary range, and expanded language structures.

 The ORANGE LEVEL presents a wide range of ideas and concepts using challenging vocabulary and complex language structures.

When sharing a book with your child, read in short stretches, pausing often to talk about the pictures. Have your child turn the pages and point to the pictures and familiar words. And be sure to reread favorite stories or parts of stories.

There is no right or wrong way to share books with children. Find time to read with your child, and pass on the legacy of literacy.

Adria F. Klein, Ph.D.
Professor Emeritus
California State University
San Bernardino, California

Editor: Christianne Jones
Designer: Amy Muehlenhardt
Page Production: Michelle Biedscheid
Art Director: Nathan Gassman
The illustrations in this book were created in watercolor and pencil.

Picture Window Books
151 Good Counsel Drive
P.O. Box 669
Mankato, MN 56002-0669
877-845-8392
www.picturewindowbooks.com

Printed in the United States of America in Stevens Point, Wisconsin.
082009
0005601R

Library of Congress Cataloging-in-Publication Data
Klein, Adria F. (Adria Fay), 1947-
Max goes to the farm / by Adria F. Klein ; illustrated by Mernie Gallagher-Cole.
p. cm. — (Read-it! readers. The life of Max)
Summary: While on a visit to his grandparents, Max and his friend DeShawn have
fun helping with the chores.
ISBN-13: 978-1-4048-3678-5 (library binding)
ISBN-10: 1-4048-3678-0 (library binding)
[1. Farms—Fiction. 2. Domestic animals—Fiction. 3. Friendship—Fiction.
4. Grandparents—Fiction.] I. Gallagher-Cole, Mernie, ill. II. Title.
PZ7.K678324Mar 2007
[E]—dc22   2007004057

Max
Goes to the
Farm

by Adria F. Klein
illustrated by Mernie Gallagher-Cole

Special thanks to our advisers for their expertise:

Adria F. Klein, Ph.D.
Professor Emeritus, California State University
San Bernardino, California

Susan Kesselring, M.A., Literacy Educator
Rosemount–Apple Valley–Eagan (Minnesota) School District

PiCTURE WiNDOW BOOKS
Minneapolis, Minnesota

Max is going to his grandparents' farm.

He invites his friend DeShawn to go to the farm.

Max and DeShawn ride horses
on a bumpy trail.

Max and DeShawn milk ten cows.

Max and DeShawn feed grain
to the pigs.

Max and DeShawn collect eggs
from the chickens.

Max and DeShawn jump into piles of hay.

Max and DeShawn are tired. They go inside for a treat.

Grandma has oatmeal cookies.

Soon it is time for Max and DeShawn
to go home.

Max and DeShawn say thank you for the fun visit.

Max wants to visit his grandparents at the farm again soon.

More *Read-it!* Readers

Bright pictures and fun stories help you practice your reading skills. Look for more books at your level.

Max Goes on the Bus

Max Goes Shopping

Max Goes to School

Max Goes to the Barber

Max Goes to the Dentist

Max Goes to the Doctor

Max Goes to the Library

Max Goes to the Playground

Max Goes to the Zoo

Max and Buddy Go to the Vet

Max and the Adoption Day Party

Max Celebrates Chinese New Year

Max Goes to a Cookout

Max Goes to the Grocery Store

Max Learns Sign Language

Max Stays Overnight

Max's Fun Day

On the Web

FactHound offers a safe, fun way to find Web sites related to this book. All of the sites on FactHound have been researched by our staff.

1. Visit www.facthound.com

2. Type in this special code:
   1404836780

3. Click on the FETCH IT button.

Your trusty FactHound will fetch the best sites for you! A complete list of *Read-it!* Readers is available on our Web site: **www.picturewindowbooks.com**